THE UNCOMMON
PRAYER-BOOK

-FANTASY AND HORROR CLASSICS-

BY

M. R. JAMES

British Library Cataloguing-in-Publication Data
A catalogue record for this book is available from the
British Library

M. R. James

Montague Rhodes James was born in Kent, England in 1862. An intellectually gifted child, he excelled academically at both Temple Grove School and Eton College before enrolling at King's College, Cambridge. A highly respected scholar to this day, James' areas of research interest were apocryphal Biblical literature and mediaeval illuminated manuscripts. He was, by turns, Fellow, Dean, and Tutor at King's College, and in 1905 was installed as Provost. James was a highly sociable man, and he travelled widely throughout Europe.

James came to writing fiction relatively late, not publishing his first collection of short stories – *Ghost Stories of an Antiquary* (1904) – until the age of 42. Many of his tales were written as Christmas Eve entertainments and read aloud to friends. James described his introduction to ghosts in 1931: "In my childhood I chanced to see a toy Punch and Judy set, with figures cut out in cardboard. One of these was The Ghost. It was a tall figure habited in white with an unnaturally long and narrow head, also surrounded with white, and a dismal visage. Upon this my conceptions of a ghost were based, and for years it permeated my dreams." James believed that must a good story must "put the reader into the position of saying to himself: 'If I'm not careful,

3

something of this kind may happen to me!'" He eventually published five collections of his ghost stories, all of which were reprinted and adapted numerous times.

Modern scholars now see James as having redefined the ghost story for the 20th century by abandoning many of the formal Gothic clichés of his predecessors and using more realistic contemporary settings. However, James's tales tend to reflect his own antiquarian interests, and he is seen as the founder of the 'antiquarian ghost story'. His first two collections – *Ghost Stories of an Antiquary* (1904) and *More Ghost Stories* (1911) – are generally regarded as his most important, containing as they do the well-known stories 'Number 13', 'Count Magnus', 'Oh, Whistle and I'll Come to You, My Lad' and 'Casting the Runes'.

The onset of World War One marked the beginning of the end of James' golden years in Cambridge. In 1918, he accepted the post of Provost of Eton College. He was awarded the Order of Merit in 1930, and died in 1936, aged 73.

THE UNCOMMON PRAYER-BOOK

Mr. Davidson was spending the first week in January alone in a country town. A combination of circumstances had driven him to that drastic course: his nearest relations were enjoying winter sports abroad, and the friends who had been kindly anxious to replace them had an infectious complaint in the house. Doubtless he might have found someone else to take pity on him; 'but,' he reflected, 'most of them have made up their parties, and after all it is only for three or four days at most that I have to fend for myself, and it will be just as well if I can get a move on with my introduction to the Leventhorp Papers. I might use the time by going down as near as I can to Gaulsford and making acquaintance with the neighbourhood. I ought to see the remains of the Leventhorp house, and the tombs in the church.'

The first day after his arrival at the Swan Hotel at Longbridge was so stormy that he got no farther than the tobacconist's. The next, comparatively bright, he used for his visit to Gaulsford, which interested him more than a little, but had no ulterior consequences. The third, which was really a pearl of a day for early January, was too fine to be spent indoors. He gathered from the landlord that a favourite practice of visitors in the summer was to take a morning train to a couple of stations westward and walk back down the valley of the Tent, through Stanford St. Thomas and

Stanford Magdalene, both of which were accounted highly picturesque villages. He closed with this plan, and we now find him seated in a third-class carriage at 9.45 a.m., on his way to Kingsbourne Junction, and studying the map of the district.

One old man was his only fellow-traveller, a piping old man, who seemed inclined for conversation. So Mr. Davidson, after going through the necessary versicles and responses about the weather, inquired whether he was going far.

'No, sir, not far, not this morning, sir,' said the old man. 'I ain't only goin' so far as what they call Kingsbourne Junction. There isn't but two stations betwixt here and there. Yes, they calls it Kingsbourne Junction.'

'I'm going there, too,' said Mr. Davidson.

'Oh indeed, sir! do you know that part?'

'No, I'm only going for the sake of taking a walk back to Longbridge, and seeing a bit of the country.'

'Oh indeed, sir! Well, 'tis a beautiful day for a gentleman as enjoys a bit of a walk.'

'Yes, to be sure. Have you got far to go when you get to Kingsbourne?'

'No, sir, I ain't got far to go, once I get to Kingsbourne Junction. I'm agoin' to see my daughter, sir. She live at Brockstone. That's about two mile across the fields from what they call Kingsbourne Junction, that is. You've got that marked down on your map, I expect, sir.'

'I expect I have. Let me see, Brockstone, did you say? Here's Kingsbourne, yes; and which way is Brockstone toward the Stanfords? Ah, I see it: Brockstone Court, in a park. I don't see the village, though.'

'No, sir, you wouldn't see no village of Brockstone. There ain't only the Court and the chapel at Brockstone.'

'Chapel? Oh yes, that's marked here too. The chapel; close by the Court, it seems to be. Does it belong to the Court?'

'Yes, sir, that's close up to the Court, only a step. Yes, that belong to the Court. My daughter, you see, sir, she's the keeper's wife now, and she live at the Court and look after things now the family's away.'

'No one living there now, then?'

'No, sir, not for a number of years. The old gentleman he lived there when I was a lad, and the lady she lived on after him to very near upon ninety years of age. And then she died, and them that have it now, they've got this other place, in Warwickshire I believe it is, and they don't do nothin' about lettin' the Court out; but Colonel Wildman he have the shooting, and young Mr. Clark, he's the agent, he come over once in so many weeks to see to things, and my daughter's husband he's the keeper.'

'And who uses the chapel? just the people round about, I suppose.'

'Oh no, no one don't use the chapel. Why, there ain't no one to go. All the people about, they go to Stanford St. Thomas Church; but my son-in-law he go to Kingsbourne Church now, because the gentleman at Stanford he have this Gregory singin', and my son-in-law he don't like that; he say he can hear the old donkey brayin' any day of the week, and he like something a little cheerful on the Sunday.' The old man drew his hand across his mouth and laughed. 'That's what my son-in-law say: he say he can hear the old donkey [etc., do copo].'

Mr. Davidson also laughed as honestly as he could, thinking meanwhile that Brockstone Court and chapel would probably be worth including in his walk, for the map showed that from Brockstone he could strike the Tent Valley quite as easily as by following the main Kingsbourne—Longbridge road. So, when the mirth excited by the remembrance of the son-in-law's bon mot had died down, he returned to the charge, and ascertained that both the Court and the chapel were of the class known as 'old-fashioned places', and that the old man would be very willing to take him thither, and his daughter would be happy to show him whatever she could.

'But that ain't a lot, sir, not as if the family was livin' there; all the lookin'-glasses is covered up, and the paintin's, and the curtains and carpets folded away: not but what I dare say she could show you a pair just to look at, because she go over them to see as the morth shouldn't get into 'em.'

'I shan't mind about that, thank you: if she can show me the inside of the chapel, that's what I'd like best to see.'

'Oh, she can show you that right enough, sir. She have the key of the door, you see, and most weeks she go in and dust about. That's a nice chapel, that is. My son-in-law he say he'll be bound they didn't have none of this Gregory singin' there. Dear! I can't help but smile when I think of him sayin' that about th' old donkey. 'I can hear him bray,' he say, 'any day of the week'; and so he can, sir, that's true, anyway.'

The walk across the fields from Kingsbourne to Brockstone was very pleasant. It lay for the most part on the top of the country, and commanded wide views over a succession of ridges, plough and pasture, or covered with dark-blue woods—all ending, more or less abruptly, on the right, in headlands that overlooked the wide valley of a great western river. The last field they crossed was bounded by a close copse, and no sooner were they in it than the path turned downwards very sharply, and it became evident that Brockstone was neatly fitted into a sudden and very narrow valley. It was not long before they had glimpses of groups of smokeless stone chimneys, and stone-tiled roofs, close beneath their feet; and not many minutes after that, they were wiping their shoes at the back door of Brockstone Court, while the keeper's dogs barked very loudly in unseen places, and Mrs. Porter in quick succession screamed at them to be quiet, greeted her father, and begged both her visitors to step in.

It was not to be expected that Mr. Davidson should escape being taken through the principal rooms of the Court, in spite of the fact that the house was entirely out of commission. Pictures, carpets, curtains, furniture, were all covered up or put away, as old Mr. Avery had said, and the admiration which our friend was very ready to bestow had to be lavished on the proportions of the rooms, and on the one painted ceiling, upon which an artist who had fled from London in the Plague-year had depicted the Triumph of Loyalty and Defeat of Sedition. In this Mr. Davidson could show an unfeigned interest. The portraits of Cromwell, Ireton, Bradshaw, Peters, and the rest, writhing in carefully-devised torments, were evidently the part of the design to which most pains had been devoted.

'That were the old Lady Sadleir had that paintin' done, same as the one what put up the chapel. They say she were the first that went up to London to dance on Oliver Cromwell's grave.' So said Mr. Avery, and continued musingly: 'Well, I suppose she got some satisfaction to 'er mind, but I don't know as I should want to pay the fare to London and back just for that, and my son-in-law he say the same: he say he don't know as he should have cared to pay all that money only for that. I was tellin' the gentleman as we come along in the train, Mary, what your 'Arry says about this Gregory singin' down at Stanford here. We 'ad a bit of a laugh over that, sir, didn't us?'

'Yes, to be sure we did; ha! ha!' Once again Mr. Davidson strove to do justice to the pleasantry of the keeper. 'But,' he said, 'if Mrs. Porter can show me the chapel, I think it should be now, for the days aren't long, and I want to get back to Longbridge before it falls quite dark.'

Even if Brockstone Court has not been illustrated in Rural Life (and I think it has not) I do not propose to point out its excellences here; but of the chapel a word must be said. It stands about a hundred yards from the house, and has its own little graveyard and trees about it. It is a stone building about seventy feet long, and in the gothic style, as that style was understood in the middle of the seventeenth century. On the whole it resembles some of the Oxford college chapels as much as anything, save that it has a distinct chancel, like a parish church, and a fanciful domed bell-turret at the south-west angle.

When the west door was thrown open, Mr. Davidson could not repress an exclamation of pleased surprise at the completeness and richness of the interior. Screen-work, pulpit, seating, and glass—all were of the same period; and as he advanced into the nave and sighted the organ-case with its gold embossed pipes in the western gallery, his cup of satisfaction was filled. The glass in the nave windows was chiefly armorial; in the chancel were figure-subjects, of the kind that may be seen at Abbey Dore, of Lord Scudamore's work. But this is not an archaeological Review.

While Mr. Davidson was still busy examining the remains of the organ (attributed to one of the Dallams, I believe) old Mr. Avery had stumped up into the chancel and was lifting the dust-cloths from the blue velvet cushions of the stalldesks—evidently it was here that the family sat. Mr. Davidson heard him say in a rather hushed tone of surprise, 'Why, Mary, here's all the books open agin!'

The reply was in a voice that sounded peevish rather than surprised. 'Tt-tt-tt, well, there, I never!'

Mrs. Porter went over to where her father was standing, and they continued talking in a lower key. Mr. Davidson saw plainly that something not quite in the common run was under discussion: so he came down the gallery stairs and joined them. There was no sign of disorder in the chancel any more than in the rest of the chapel, which was beautifully clean, but the eight folio Prayer–Books on the cushions of the stall-desks were indubitably open.

Mrs. Porter was inclined to be fretful over it. 'Whoever can it be as does it?' she said, 'for there's no key but mine, nor yet door but the one we come in by, and the winders is barred, every one of 'em: I don't like it, father, that I don't.'

'What is it, Mrs. Porter? Anything wrong?' said Mr. Davidson.

'No, sir, nothing reely wrong, only these books. Every time pretty near that I come in to do up the place, I shuts 'em and spreads the cloths over 'em to keep off the dust, ever since Mr. Clark spoke about it when I first come; and yet there they are again, and always the same page—and as I says, whoever it can be as does it with the door and winders shut; and as I says, it makes anyone feel queer comin' in here alone as I 'ave to do, not as I'm given that way myself, not to be frightened easy, I mean to say; and there's not a rat in the place—not as no rat wouldn't trouble to do a thing like that, do you think, sir?'

'Hardly, I should say; but it sounds very queer. Are they always open at the same place, did you say?'

'Always the same place, sir, one of the psalms it is, and I didn't particular notice it the first time or two, till I see a little red line of printing, and it's always caught my eye since.'

Mr. Davidson walked along the stalls and looked at the open books. Sure enough, they all stood at the same page: Psalm cix, and at the head of it, just between the number and the Dens Iaudem, was a rubric, 'For the 25th day of April'. Without pretending to minute knowledge of the history of the Book of Common Prayer, he knew enough to be sure that this was a very odd and wholly unauthorized addition to its text; and though he remembered that April is St. Mark's Day, he could not imagine what appropriateness this very savage psalm could have to that festival. With slight misgivings, he ventured to turn over the leaves to examine the title-page, and knowing the need for particular accuracy in these matters, he devoted some ten minutes to making a line-for-line transcript of it. The date was 1653; the printer called himself Anthony Cadman. He turned to the list of Proper Psalms for certain days: yes, added to it was that same inexplicable entry: For the 25th day of April: the moth Psalm. An expert would no doubt have thought of many other points to inquire into, but this antiquary, as I have said, was no expert. He took stock, however, of the binding, a handsome one of tooled blue leather, bearing the arms that figured in several of the nave windows in various combinations.

'How often,' he said at last to Mrs. Porter, 'have you found these books lying open like this?'

'Reely I couldn't say, sir, but it's a great many times now. Do you recollect, father, me telling you about it the first time I noticed it?'

'That I do, my dear: you was in a rare taking, and I don't so much wonder at it; that was five year ago I was paying you a visit at Michaelmas time, and you come in at tea-time, and says you, 'Father, there's the books layin' open under the cloths agin'; and I didn't know what my daughter was speakin' about, you see, sir, and I says, 'Books?' just like that, I says; and then it all came out. But as Harry says,—that's my son-in-law, sir,—'whoever it can be,' he says, 'as does it, because there ain't only the one door, and we keeps the key locked up,' he says, 'and the winders is barred, every one on 'em. Well,' he says, 'I lay once I could catch 'em at it they wouldn't do it a second time,' he says. And no more they wouldn't, I don't believe, sir. Well that was five year ago, and it's been happenin' constant ever since by your account, my dear. Young Mr. Clark he don't seem to think much to it, but then he don't live here, you see, and 'tisn't his business to come and clean up here of a dark afternoon, is it?'

'I suppose you never notice anything else odd when you are at work here, Mrs. Porter?' said Mr. Davidson.

'No, sir, I do not,' said Mrs. Porter, 'and it's a funny thing to me I don't, with the feeling I have as there's someone settin' here—no, it's the other side, just within the screen—and lookin' at me all the time I'm dustin' in the gallery and pews. But I never yet see nothin' worse than myself, as the sayin' goes, and I kindly hope I never may.'

In the conversation that followed (there was not much of it) nothing was added to the statement of the case. Having parted on good terms with Mr. Avery and his daughter, Mr. Davidson addressed himself to his eight-mile walk. The little valley of Brockstone soon led him down into the broader one of the Tent, and on to Stanford St. Thomas, where he found refreshment.

We need not accompany him all the way to Longbridge.

But as he was changing his socks before dinner, he suddenly paused and said half-aloud, 'By Jove, that is a rum thing!' It had not occurred to him before how strange it was that any edition of the Prayer–Book should have been issued in 1653, seven years before the Restoration, five years before Cromwell's death, and when the use of the book, let alone the printing of it, was penal. He must have been a bold man who put his name and a date on that title-page. Only, Mr. Davidson reflected, it probably was not his name at all, for the ways of printers in difficult times were devious.

As he was in the front hall of the Swan that evening, making some investigations about trains, a small motor stopped in front of the door, and out of it came a small man in a fur coat, who stood on the steps and gave directions in a rather yapping foreign accent to his chauffeur. When he came into the hotel, he was seen to be black-haired and pale-faced, with a little pointed beard, and gold pince-nez; altogether, very neatly turned out.

He went to his room, and Mr. Davidson saw no more of him till dinner-time. As they were the only two dining that night, it was not difficult for the newcomer to find an excuse for falling into talk; he was evidently wishing to make out what brought Mr. Davidson into that neighbourhood at that season.

'Can you tell me how far it is from here to Arlingworth?' was one of his early questions, and it was one which threw some light on his own plans, for Mr. Davidson recollected having seen at the station an advertisement of a sale at Arlingworth Hall, comprising old furniture, pictures, and books. This, then, was a London dealer.

'No,' he said, 'I've never been there. I believe it lies out by Kingsbourne—it can't be less than twelve miles. I see there's a sale there shortly.'

The other looked at him inquisitively, and he laughed. 'No,' he said, as if answering a question, 'you needn't be afraid of my competing; I'm leaving this place tomorrow.'

This cleared the air, and the dealer, whose name was Homberger, admitted that he was interested in books, and thought there might be in these old country-house libraries something to repay a journey. 'For,' said he, 'we English have always this marvellous talent for accumulating rarities in the most unexpected places, ain't it?'

And in the course of the evening he was most interesting on the subject of finds made by himself and others. 'I shall take the occasion after this sale to look round the district a bit: perhaps you could inform me of some likely spots, Mr. Davidson?' But Davidson, though he had seen some very tempting locked-up bookcases at Brockstone Court, kept his counsel. He did not really like Mr. Homberger.

Next day, as he sat in the train, a little ray of light came to illuminate one of yesterday's puzzles. He happened to take out an almanac-diary that he had bought for the new year, and it occurred to him to look at the remarkable events for April 25. There it was: 'St Mark. Oliver Cromwell born, 1599.'

That, coupled with the painted ceiling, seemed to explain a good deal. The figure of old Lady Sadleir became more substantial to his imagination, as of one in whom love for Church and King had gradually given place to intense hate of the power that had silenced the one and slaughtered the other. What curious evil service was that which she and a few like her had been wont to celebrate year by year in that remote valley? and how in the world had she managed to elude authority? And again, did not this persistent opening of the books agree oddly with the other traits of her portrait known to him?

It would be interesting for anyone who chanced to be near Brockstone on the twenty-fifth of April to look in at the chapel and see if anything exceptional happened. When he came to think of it, there seemed to be no reason why he should not be that person himself: he, and if possible, some congenial friend. He resolved that so it should be.

Knowing that he knew really nothing about the printing of Prayer-Books, he realized that he must make it his business to get the best light on the matter without divulging his reasons. I may say at once that his search was entirely fruitless. One writer of the early part of the nineteenth century, a writer of rather windy and rhapsodical chat about books, professed to have heard of a special anti-Cromwellian issue of the Prayer–Book in the very midst of the Commonwealth period. But he did not claim to have seen a copy, and no one had believed him. Looking into this matter, Mr. Davidson found that the statement was based on letters from a correspondent who had lived near Longbridge: so he was inclined to think that the Brockstone Prayer–Books were at the bottom of it, and had excited a momentary interest.

Months went on, and St. Mark's Day came near. Nothing interfered with Mr. Davidson's plans of visiting Brockstone, or with those of the friend whom he had persuaded to go with him, and to whom alone he had confided the puzzle. The same 9.45 train which had taken him in January took them now to Kingsbourne; the same field-path led them to Brock-stone. But today they stopped more than once to pick a cowslip; the distant woods and ploughed uplands were of another colour, and in the copse there was, as Mrs. Porter said, 'a regular charm of birds; why you couldn't hardly collect your mind sometimes with it.'

She recognized Mr. Davidson at once and was very ready to do the honours of the chapel. The new visitor, Mr. Witham, was as much struck by the completeness of it as Mr. Davidson had been. 'There can't be such another in England,' he said.

'Books open again, Mrs. Porter?' said Davidson, as they

walked up to the chancel.

'Dear, yes, I expect so, sir,' said Mrs. Porter, as she drew off the cloths. 'Well, there!' she exclaimed the next moment, 'if they ain't shut! That's the first time ever I've found 'em so. But it's not for want of care on my part, I do assure you, gentlemen, if they wasn't, for I felt the cloths the last thing before I shut up last week, when the gentleman had done photografting the heast winder, and every one was shut, and where there was ribbons left I tied 'em. Now I think of it, I don't remember ever to 'ave done that before, and per'aps, whoever it is it just made the difference to 'em. Well, it only shows, don't it? If at first you don't succeed, try, try, try again.'

Meanwhile the two men had been examining the books, and now Davidson spoke.

'I'm sorry to say I'm afraid there's something wrong here, Mrs. Porter. These are not the same books.'

It would make too long a business to detail all Mrs. Porter's outcries, and the questionings that followed. The upshot was this. Early in January the gentleman had come to see over the chapel and thought a great deal of it and said he must come back in the spring weather and take some photografts. And only a week ago he had drove up in his motoring car, and a very 'eavy box with the slides in it, and she had locked him in because he said something about a long explosion, and she was afraid of some damage happening: and he says, no, not explosion, but it appeared the lantern what they take the slides with worked very slow, and so he was in there the best part of an hour and she come and let him out, and he drove off with his box and all and gave her his visiting-card, and oh, dear, dear, to think of such a thing! he must have changed the books and took the old ones away with him in his box.

'What sort of man was he?'

'Oh, dear, he was a small-made gentleman, if you can call him so after the way he've behaved, with black hair, that is if it was hair, and gold eye-glasses, if they was gold: reely, one don't know what to believe. Sometimes I doubt he weren't a reel Englishman at all, and yet he seemed to know the language, and had the name on his visiting-card like anybody else might.

'Just so; might we see the card? Yes: T. W. Henderson, and an address somewhere near Bristol. Well, Mrs. Porter, it's quite plain this Mr. Henderson, as he calls himself, has walked off with your eight Prayer-Books and put eight others about the same size in place of them. Now listen to me. I suppose you must tell your husband about this, but neither you nor he must say one word about it to anyone else. If you'll give me the address of the agent—Mr. Clark, isn't it?—I will write to him and tell him exactly what has happened, and that it really is no fault of yours. But, you understand, we must keep it very quiet: and why? Because this man who has stolen the books will of course try to sell them one at a time—for I may tell you they are worth a good deal of money—and the only way we can bring it home to him is by keeping a sharp look out and saying nothing.'

By dint of repeating the same advice in various forms they succeeded in impressing Mrs. Porter with the real need for silence, and were forced to make a concession only in the case of Mr. Avery, who was expected on a visit shortly: 'But you may be safe with father, sir,' said Mrs. Porter. 'Father ain't a talkin' man.'

It was not quite Mr. Davidson's experience of him; still, there were no neighbours at Brockstone, and even Mr. Avery must be aware that gossip with anybody on such a subject would be likely to end in the Porters having to look out for another situation.

A last question was whether Mr. Henderson, so-called, had anyone with him.

'No, sir, not when he come he hadn't: he was working his own motoring car himself, and what luggage he had, let me see: there was his lantern and this box of slides inside the carriage, which I helped him into the chapel and out of it myself with it, if only I'd knowed! And as he drove away under the big yew tree by the monument I see the long white bundle laying on the top of the coach, what I didn't notice when he drove up. But he set in front, sir, and only the boxes inside behind him. And do you reely think, sir, as his name weren't Henderson at all? Oh dear me, what a dreadful thing! Why fancy what trouble it might bring to a innocent person that might never have set foot in the place but for that!'

They left Mrs. Porter in tears. On the way home there was much discussion as to the best means of keeping watch upon possible sales. What Henderson–Homberger (for there could be no real doubt of the identity) had done was, obviously, to bring down the requisite number of folio Prayer-Books—disused copies from college chapels and the like, bought ostensibly for the sake of the bindings, which were superficially like enough to the old ones—and to substitute them at his leisure for the genuine articles. A week had now passed without any public notice being taken of the theft. He would take a little time himself to find out about the rarity of the books, and would ultimately, no doubt, 'place' them cautiously. Between them, Davidson and Witham were in a position to know a good deal of what was passing in the book-world, and they could map out the ground pretty completely. A weak point with them at the moment was that neither of them knew under what other name or names Henderson–Homberger carried on business. But there are ways of solving these problems.

And yet all this planning proved unnecessary.

We are transported to a London office on this same 25th of April. We find there, within closed doors, late in the day, two police inspectors, a commissionaire, and a youthful clerk. The two latter, both rather pale and agitated in appearance, are sitting on chairs and being questioned.

'How long do you say you've been in this Mr. Poschwitz's employment? Six months? And what was his business? Attended sales in various parts and brought home parcels of books. Did he keep a shop anywhere? No? Disposed of 'em here and there, and sometimes to private collectors. Right. Now then, when did he go out last? Rather better than a week ago. Tell you where he was going? No? Said he was going to start next day from his private residence, and shouldn't be at the office—that's here, eh?—before two days: you was to attend as usual. Where is his private residence? Oh, that's the address, Norwood way; I see. Any family? Not in this country? Now, then, what account do you give of what's happened since he came back? Came back on the Tuesday, did he? and this is the Saturday. Bring any books? One package: where is it? In the safe: you got the key? No, to be sure, it's open, of course. How did he seem when he got back—cheerful? Well, but how do you mean curious? Thought he might be in for an illness: he said that, did he? Odd smell got in his nose, couldn't get rid of it: told you to let him know who wanted to see him before you let 'em in? That wasn't usual with him? Much the same all Wednesday, Thursday, Friday. Out a good deal; said he was going to the British Museum. Often went there to make inquiries in the

way of his business. Walked up and down a lot in the office
when he was in? Anyone call in on those days? Mostly when
he was out. Anyone find him in? Oh, Mr. Collinson? Who's
Mr. Collinson? An old customer: know his address? All right,
give it us afterwards. Well, now, what about this morning?
You left Mr. Poschwitz's here at twelve and went home.
Anybody see you? Commissionaire, you did? Remained at
home till summoned here. Very well.

'Now commissionaire; we have your name—Watkins.
eh? Very well, make your statement: don't go too quick, so
as we can get it down.'

'I was on duty 'ere later than usual, Mr. Potwitch
'axing asked me to remain on, and ordered his lunching
to be sent in, which come as ordered. I was in the lobby
from eleven-thirty on, and see Mr. Bligh [the clerk] leave
at about twelve. After that no one come in at all except Mr.
Potwitch's lunching come at one o'clock and the man left
in five minutes' time. Towards the afternoon I became tired
of waitin' and I come upstairs to this first floor. The outer
door what lead to the orfice stood open, and I come up to
the plate-glass door here. Mr. Potwitch he was standing
behind the table smoking a cigar, and he laid it down on the
mantelpiece and felt in his trouser pockets and took out a
key and went across to the safe. And I knocked on the glass,
thinkin' to see if he wanted me to come and take away his
tray, but he didn't take no notice, bein' engaged with the safe

door. Then he got it open and stooped down and seemed to be lifting up a package off of the floor of the safe. And then, sir, I see what looked to be like a great roll of old shabby white flannel about four to five feet high fall for'ards out of the inside of the safe right against Mr. Potwitch's shoulder as he was stooping over: and Mr. Porwitch he raised himself up as it were, resting his hands on the package, and give a exclamation. And I can't hardly expect you should take what I says, bur as true as I stand here I see this roll had a kind of a face in the upper end of it, sir. You can't be more surprised than what I was, I can assure you, and I've seen a lot in me time...Yes, I can describe it if you wish it, sir: it was very much the same as this wall here in colour [the wall had an earth-coloured distemper] and it had a bit of a band tied round underneath, and the eyes, well they was dry-like, and much as if there was two big spiders' bodies in the holes...Hair? no, I don't know as there was much hair to be seen: the flannel-stuff was over the top of the 'ead...I'm very sure it warn't what it should have been. No, I only see it in a flash, but I took it in like a photograft—wish I hadn't... Yest, sir, it fell right over on to Mr. Pot-witch's shoulder, and this face hid in his neck—yes, sir, about where the injury was—more like a ferret goin' for a rabbit than anythink else, and he rolled over, and of course I tried to get in at the door, but as you know, sir, it were locked on the inside, and all I could do, I rung up everyone, and the surgeon come, and the police and you gentlemen, and you know as much as what I do. If you won't be requirin' me any more today I'd be glad to be get tin' off home: it's shook me up more than I thought for.'

'Well.' said one of the inspectors, when they were left alone, and 'Well?' said the other inspector: and, after a pause, 'What's the surgeon's report again? You've got it there. Yes. Effect on the blood like the worst kind of snake-bite: death almost instantaneous. I'm glad of that for his sake; he was a nasty sight. No case for detaining this man Watkins, anyway; we know all about him. And what about this safe, now? We'd better go over it again, and, by the way, we haven't opened that package he was busy with when he died.'

'Well, handle it careful,' said the other. 'There might be this snake in it, for what you know. Get a light into the corners of the place, too. Well: there's room for a shortish person to stand up in; but what about ventilation?'

'Perhaps,' said the other slowly, as he explored the safe with an electric torch, 'perhaps they didn't require much of that. My word! it strikes warm coming out of that place! like a vault, it is. But here, what's this bank-like of dust all spread out into the room? That must have come there since the door was opened; it would sweep it all away if you moved it—see? Now what do you make of that?'

'Make of it? About as much as I make of anything else in this case. One of London's mysteries this is going to be, by what I can see, and I don't believe a photographer's box full of large-size old fashioned Prayer–Books is going to take us much further. For that's just what your package is.'

It was a natural but hasty utterance. The preceding narrative shows that there was in fact plenty of material for constructing a case; and when once Messrs, Davidson and Witham had brought their end to Scotland Yard, the join-up was soon made, and the circle completed.

To the relief of Mrs. Porter, the owners of Brockstone decided not to replace the books in the chapel: they repose, I believe, in a safe-deposit in town. The police have their own methods of keeping certain matters out of the newspapers: otherwise it can hardly be supposed that Watkins's evidence about Mr. Poschwitz's death could have failed to furnish a good many headlines of a startling character to the press.